Avatar

by Melaina Faranda
illustrated by Renée Nault

contents

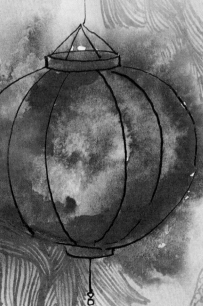

Clarify   taunting

Predict
What do you think this story will be about? What helped you form your opinion?

Predators

A sudden sharp pain made him stop. **But there was no time.** Not if he wanted to get away from them with only a big black bruise. He should never have tried to defend Lan. Kevin was used to being picked on, but it had made his blood boil to see them taunting her. When she finally put her book down, he had seen tears glistening in her dark, crescent-moon eyes.

Kevin was used to being picked on

Visual Features

How do the visual images and design reflect the text content on this page? What feelings do they evoke?

The stone that had hit his neck now winked evilly from a grimy plastic bag snagged on the parched grass. Kevin stared at the stone's razor edge.

WHAT WOULD HAVE HAPPENED IF IT HAD HIT HIS HEAD?

Shuddering, he put his hand to the back of his neck and felt the roughess of grazed skin.

Language Features

Simile/Metaphor/ Personification
What literary devices has the author used? What was her purpose for using these devices? How did they help your understanding of the events?

they were circling the edge of the vacant lot like hungry wolves

They'd taken his cap. Jamie had rubbed it into dog droppings on the vacant lot. Then the three boys had chased after him, waving the cap and yelling abuse.

"COME BACK HERE AND STICK YOUR HAT ON, FAT BOY!"

Kevin jolted into action. Stumbling on, he rounded the corner and hurtled along a street of identical brick houses.

Beyond the Text

Can you relate to how Kevin feels when the boys rub his cap in the dog droppings? What connections can you make to the issue of bullying?

Behind him, they were circling the edge of the vacant lot like hungry wolves. He could still hear them calling.

Kevin passed Mrs Delaney's garden, with its gnomes and ceramic snails and tyre swans, and then the Azzapardis'. Mrs Azzapardi was out the front, hosing the concrete beneath the grape trellis. The dusty smell of wet cement filled Kevin's nostrils. She pointed a plump arm in his direction and a jet of icy water sprayed all over him. "Why you runneeng when eet ees so 'ot?"

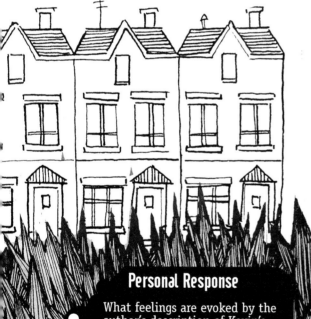

Personal Response

What feelings are evoked by the author's description of Kevin's bag being dunked in the toilet?

Kevin shook his head and, like a dog, furiously flicked off the water. He wasn't hot any more, but now his school books would be soaked. He'd be in trouble again at school. At least this time it was only tap water. A week ago, his bag had been dunked in a toilet.

The Game

The house was empty. He'd known it would be. Luckily, Jamie and his cronies didn't. Kevin tugged out the key he kept on a bit of string around his neck. He couldn't leave it in his school bag or pocket. Anything could happen to it.

THE HOUSE WAS FAST BECOMING **THE ONLY** PLACE HE WAS SAFE.

But Kevin knew that it was only a matter of time before they attacked the house.

A sickly wave of perfume and stale cigarettes enveloped him the moment he opened the door. She had been home this morning.

Kevin peered through the open door of his mother's bedroom. On her dressing table, one of her many lipsticks had been carelessly left open. Its scarlet gleamed wetly in the light filtering through the sheet tacked over the window. Sighing, Kevin replaced the cap on the lipstick and continued to the kitchen.

Inside the fridge were rows of chocolate bars, half a carton of off milk and the leftovers from last night's takeaway. Kevin grabbed a chocolate bar and went to his room.

Neon lights glowed in the darkness, welcoming him. Kevin threw his bag down and switched on the computer. The gentle hum of its start-up instantly soothed him. As he typed in the name of the game, a roar of adrenalin filled him. A tall, heavily muscled figure with depthless eyes and a rock-like jaw grinned back at him. Himself. In the real world. His avatar.

"What is our mission today?" the avatar droned.

Kevin smiled and leaned back into his chair. He typed in with two fingers, "We must fly over the wastelands to fight the evil Jamaster and rescue Princess Lana."

The avatar raised his sword and whistled for their war chariot. Kevin had painstakingly fashioned it from a mix of World War II fighter planes and the latest high-tech space shuttles.

he wished he could stay in this world forever

Setting

How effectively has the author developed the mood and atmosphere of Kevin's home? What can you infer from the setting about his family circumstances?

"It will be a pleasure," the avatar intoned.

"A pleasure," Kevin agreed. Already he felt taller, stronger, powerful. As he mentally hopped into the craft with his avatar, he wished he could stay in this world forever.

Inference

What inferences can you make about Kevin's wish that he could stay in the cyber world forever?

Clarify   adrenalin
painstakingly
high-tech

7

Sanctuary

Kevin's heart pounded. Jamie and the others slunk towards him from behind B Block.

HE QUICKENED HIS PACE AND SLIPPED, JUST IN TIME, THROUGH SLIDING GLASS DOORS into sanctuary.

Mr O'Dowd looked up from a book catalogue and gave a brief nod of recognition. Kevin had become a regular in the lunchtime huddle of library kids.

Jamie and the others barged in behind him noisily.

Mr O'Dowd raised his gingery eyebrows and tapped impatiently on the counter. "Are you boys looking for anything in particular?"

Jamie darted Kevin a narrow-eyed promise of later pain. "Come on," he ordered his two mates, "let's get out of nerd central."

Kevin drifted through the long, quiet rows of books. History, Science, Biography, Mythology, Technology… He wondered if he should have simply let Jamie thump him rather than carry this sickening dread. Yesterday afternoon and evening, he had taken great satisfaction in letting the avatar take revenge on Jamaster. Kevin had been thrilled by the fury of the avatar's attack. Then, rescuing Princess Lana, it had been impossible to stop his avatar from kissing her…

Heat rose in Kevin's cheeks at the memory of how she had clung to him, her long silk dress swirling around their feet. Her beautiful black hair had billowed out into the rosy cyber sunset as she had kissed him again and murmured, "Kevin…"

Reading Between the Lines

How do you think ongoing bullying affects people? What effect has bullying had on Kevin?

Jamie darted Kevin
a narrow-eyed promise
of later again

Opinion

What is your
stance on the
issue of bullying?
What action can
people take to
prevent it? Do you
think your school
deals effectively/
ineffectively
with bullying?
Why?

Clarify sanctuary
nerd central
mythology

Secret Names

"Kevin?"

Kevin was jolted out of his pleasant daydream. Lan sat curled on a seat next to him with a brick-sized dictionary.

He blushed. "Oh…er…hi."

Ever since Lan had first arrived at school, he had longed to talk to her. In History, he sat at the desk directly behind hers. While Ms Janaki droned on, he stared at Lan's shiny black hair and her neat, delicate earlobes with their tiny dragon earrings.

Now Kevin wished again that he could be more like his avatar. He wanted to impress her. Avatar would be smooth and in control and know what to say. But this was the school library and he was only a fat boy who had no idea how to make her like him.

"Thank you for defending me yesterday," Lan said quietly.

Clarify
droned
impress
solemn

At the memory of her silent tears, Kevin's fists bunched by his sides. He could feel the rough edges of his bitten-down nails digging into his palms. "Don't listen to them. They're pigs."

Lan burst into laughter.

"What's so funny?" Kevin asked, hoping she wasn't laughing at him.

Lan's dark eyes became solemn. "I am sorry. But in my country there are many pigs in the street. They have such little eyes and hairy skin. Like Jamie."

Kevin smiled. "What is your country like?" he asked. He had been intrigued from the moment Ms Janaki had clucked around Lan and introduced her to the class as a "special new student all the way from Vietnam".

Beyond the Text

What connections can you make to Kevin's desire to impress Lan?

"Noisy," Lan said. "There are people everywhere, cooking and selling things. Animals wander around the streets."

"Pigs?" Kevin asked with a grin.

Lan nodded. "And dogs and ducks. And there are dragons," she added dreamily.

"BEAUTIFUL DRAGONS WITH PRECIOUS STONES UNDER THEIR TONGUES.

Dragons that can breathe fire or water."

"Dragons?" Kevin repeated. He hoped she wasn't trying to make a fool of him.

"Ones made of red silk and gold paper," Lan said. "We can only have power over them if we know their secret names."

Kevin thought about the silent suburban streets surrounding the school, without dragons or ducks or people. "Why did you come here?"

The sparkle in Lan's eyes faded. Her dark gaze was haunted. "My parents say it isn't safe there. We left two years ago. After my brother stepped on a landmine."

Author Purpose

Why do you think the author wrote about Lan's happy memories of her homeland and then introduced the sad memories of losing her brother to a landmine? What message is the author conveying to the reader here?

Siren Call

Without thinking, Kevin reached out to pat her shoulder. He couldn't imagine what she must feel like.

"Going to kiss her, fat boy?"

Kevin swivelled.

Jamie leered at them from between two tall metal bookshelves.

Clarify etiquette
humiliated
sucker bait

Visual Features

What effects do the design and visual images on this spread have on you? How do these features influence your response to the story?

Opinion

Do you think the student teacher should have taken some action when Jamie belted Kevin in the guts? Why/why not? What would you have done in the same circumstances?

e was going to a place where he could be strong

Mr O'Dowd was no longer behind the counter. A single supervising student teacher was banging the photocopier lid up and down.

"Leave us alone," Kevin muttered.

"Yeah? Who's gonna make me?" Lunging like a beast of prey, Jamie belted him in the guts.

Kevin bent double, groaning.

Analyse

"Kevin heard the silent siren call of the game. He was going to a place where he could be strong. Powerful. Invincible"

What inferences can you make about the impact computer games have on Kevin's life? Could this impact have serious consequences? What is your opinion?

"Like punching a cushion," Jamie said disgustedly. "You big tub of lard."

"Leave him," Lan cried. "You go away." She hastened to Kevin and put her arm around him. "Miss! Miss!" she shouted.

At the far end of the library, the student teacher looked up, saw Jamie, sighed and then looked away.

"Right, young man." Mr O'Dowd appeared at last. He looked at Jamie as if he were something to be wiped off his shoe. "Unless you intend to borrow a book about social etiquette, get out. Now."

Jamie rolled his eyes. "Later," he mouthed to Kevin, before slouching back out of the library.

"ARE YOU OKAY?" LAN ASKED WORRIEDLY.

Kevin shrugged, humiliated by the way he had crumpled in front of her. He gave a short laugh. "Sure. I have to go." There was no way he was hanging around like sucker bait until school finished.

He sneaked out through the back of the school, past the scabby pine trees and through the shopping centre car park. More than ever, Kevin heard the silent siren call of the game. He was going to a place where he could be strong. Powerful. Invincible.

Jamaster

Avatar left the warship parked in the vast hangars of his space palace. Instead, he rode a scarlet and gold dragon. It had the head of a camel, bulbous demon eyes, the twisting body of a snake and a tiger's claws. They winged their way swiftly to Jamaster's realm.

He must be PUNISHED.

Flying over vast purple rivers and spiky mountains that spewed golden fire, they reached the deadened black earth of Jamaster's kingdom. It was a hellish place, spewing sulphurous yellow-green smoke. Winged hybrid cyber creatures spat and shot target-seeking barbs into intruders.

Effortlessly, they repelled these creatures with multiple eyes and strange, spiked heads. Avatar blighted them with his sword. The dragon breathed ice to make the creatures freeze, so that they dropped like grotesque statues onto the festering land beneath.

Jamaster's castle was a circle of shining black metal. Avatar laughed at the evil lord's minions with their piggy snouts and beady red eyes. He slashed at them with his sword. "Here, piggy, piggy!"

Avatar waded through the carnage. Jamaster was hiding in the inner chamber, clutching Princess Lana with one hand. With the other, Jamaster pressed a razor-fine lightblade to her throat. "Drop your weapon. Any closer and…" Jamaster smiled nastily and looked pointedly at the lightblade.

Lana's eyes widened with terror.

Clarify realm grotesque
sulphurous festering
hybrid minions
blighted

14

Dragon Tears

Avatar reluctantly lowered his sword.

Jamaster laughed. "Weak," he sneered. "Weak as…"

The chamber erupted. Shards flew about the room as a scarlet and gold dragon burst in, flexing its sabre-like claws.

The princess leapt away from where Jamaster had fallen to the ground and raced to the dragon.

The dragon and the girl looked at each other intently. She whispered its secret name.

Instantly, the dragon's tongue unfurled like a long red ribbon. Princess Lana reached in. She drew out a sparkling diamond the size of a small duck's egg or a dragon's tear.

Avatar put his powerful arms around her slender waist. She craned her face up to meet his and…

"Kevvy, sweetie, IS THAT YOU?"

What was she doing home? Kevin cursed and turned off the screen just as his door flew open.

Beyond the Text

"When would she [Mum] learn to live in the real world?" **What other character could you apply the same comment to in a parallel situation?**

Clarify   sabre-like
unfurled

16

His mother wore a faded sweatshirt and tracksuit pants instead of her usual tight jeans and low-cut blouses. Her lips looked weirdly pale and her mascara had run, making her sad brown eyes like those of a frightened animal.

> Kevin guessed that she'd broken up with the latest guy even before his mother said dully, "Dave ended it. He didn't think I was the one…"

Kevin moved forward and awkwardly hugged her.

"Why doesn't it ever work out?" she moaned. "What's wrong with me? All I ever wanted was to find my Prince Charming. My soul mate…"

Kevin closed his eyes, DREADING what always came next.

"Dave's just like your father," she hissed. "No good. Your father left me as soon as you came along."

He couldn't bear it. He had to get away. "Mum. I'll go get some takeout. Pizza?" He knew she'd only pick off the pineapple bits and he'd get to eat the pizza by himself.

"I'm sick of pizza. Get me something different."

Kevin fled into the night.

Dave hadn't been the one. Same with Frank and Giovanni and Paul and all the others with their fast, flashy cars.

When would she learn to LIVE IN THE REAL WORLD?

Reading Between the Lines

What inferences can you make about the relationship between Kevin and his mum?

Personal Response

What feelings are evoked by the author's description of the emotional distress experienced by Mum and Kevin?

Strange Song

White streetlights glared down on Mrs Delaney's tyre swans and sprinklers ticked over squares of lawn. Warm smells of cooking wafted out onto the road. It made Kevin even hungrier as he trudged along to a strip of takeaway shops he rarely visited.

The enticing aroma of hamburgers and frying chips drew Kevin into the first shop. Instantly, he ducked out of sight.

Jamie and his mates were playing the **old-style pinball** machines.

A few shops up was a restaurant with red and gold plastic fans arranged across a ledge. An octagonal mirror flashed above the entrance.

There was a rush of spicy air as the door opened.

"Kevin!"

"Oh…hi."

Lan looked older than she did at school. She wore her hair up and a narrow red satin dress that buttoned at the side. Lan smiled. "Come and meet my family."

Visual Features

What effects do the visual images and design have on you? Why do you think the illustrator used warm colours in this image? How do these features influence your response to the story?

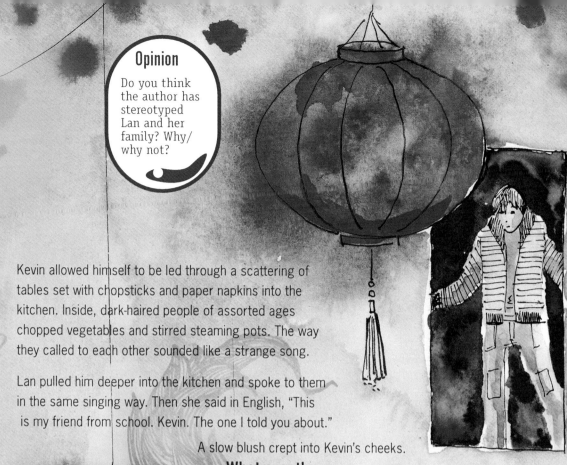

Opinion

Do you think the author has stereotyped Lan and her family? Why/why not?

Kevin allowed himself to be led through a scattering of tables set with chopsticks and paper napkins into the kitchen. Inside, dark-haired people of assorted ages chopped vegetables and stirred steaming pots. The way they called to each other sounded like a strange song.

Lan pulled him deeper into the kitchen and spoke to them in the same singing way. Then she said in English, "This is my friend from school. Kevin. The one I told you about."

A slow blush crept into Kevin's cheeks.

What exactly HAD SHE TOLD THEM ABOUT HIM?

Whatever it was, it must have been good, because they all beamed at him. Even the toothless old lady shelling prawns.

"They like you," Lan said, pleased. "My grandmother says you must eat. What would you like?"

This wasn't going to be a place that sold burgers. He had never eaten Vietnamese food before.

Seeing his confusion, Lan's eyes grew mischievous. "What about pork rolls?"

19

The Unfriendlies

Kevin shivered. A gust of cold night air bit into his cheeks. Clutching a container of food for his mother, he glanced back. The mirror above the restaurant door sparkled in the streetlight. Lan had said it was to stop unfriendly dragons from entering.

Kevin longed to return to the spicy warmth of the restaurant. The pork rolls had been delicious. But best of all had been Lan's family's eagerness to include him. Even her grandmother had insisted on showing him the best way to make ginger prawn salad.

It had made HIM FEEL HAPPIER than he could ever remember.

...y were waiting for him

Plot

Has the plot been convincing/unconvincing in your opinion? What do you think will happen in the conclusion of the story?

20

A low hiss made him spin around. Beyond the perimeter of the streetlight were three bunched-up shadows.

They were waiting for him.

Kevin tried to run, but happiness and a full stomach had made him slow.

They grabbed him and pulled him into the shadows, against a prickly hedge.

"**Been** WITH YOUR **girlfriend?**" Jamie taunted.

He pulled his eyes into slits with his fingers, then pushed Kevin straight into the arms of one of his thugs.

"Don't you say a word about her!" Kevin shouted. "You leave Lan out of this. If you want to pick on someone, pick on me."

"My pleasure," Jamie said.

Character Analysis

Summarise what you know about the characters, using evidence from the text and the inferences you have made.

Clarify cowering
prone
writhing

they'll never
hurt you or me again

Symbolism

What is the significance of Avatar
to Kevin? What connections can you
make to the underlying meaning?

Avatar's Revenge

Jamie jabbed a fist into Kevin's ribs and he grunted with pain.

With the next blow, he dropped the food for his mother. There was a wet, garlicky slap of rice noodles and prawns.

When he saw Lan's grandmother's food slicked over the pavement, Kevin's pain gave way to fury. Like a volcano, it forced its way up and erupted. He felt as if his body was changing. Pure, raw energy stiffened the loose flesh on his arms and legs and tightened his gut.

AVATAR. He was all-powerful, INVINCIBLE.

Jamie backed away, his piggy eyes round with fear.

Kevin reached forward. He had no need of a sword. Instead, he grabbed Jamie's shoulders and shook him effortlessly until his head went floppy. He reached next for Jamie's cowering companions. As he tripped one over his leg, he heard a satisfying crunch. The other one didn't wait.

"Kevin!" Lan called from the entrance to the restaurant. She raced over, followed by her family. When Lan saw Jamie's prone body, and the other boy writhing in pain, she gave a small scream. "What happened?"

Another surge of power burned through him.

He was no longer fat, bumbling Kevin. He was Avatar. He wanted to grab the girl and crush her close to him. He had conquered. He was the victor.

Lan backed away. It was as if she didn't recognise him. Her family clustered around, moaning with distress. The gold dragons in Lan's ears seemed mottled and dull in the streetlight.

"I won," Kevin said. "Can't you see? I won. They'll never hurt you or me again."

"Go," Lan said simply, her eyes tired and sad. "Go."

Kevin strode through the streets as if he owned them. There was nothing and no one to be afraid of now. He kicked at Mrs Delaney's yappy little terrier and pulled a bunch of grapes from Mrs Azzapardi's trellis. He threw the grapes into his mouth, one by one.

When he reached home, Kevin saw that his mother had crashed out in front of the television. Usually, he would have helped her into bed or laid a blanket over her. Now, he felt pitiless. She was such a victim. Why didn't she just seize hold of the things she wanted and destroy the things she didn't?

Reading Between the Lines

What do you think underpins the great distress of Lan and her family over Kevin's violent outburst?

Teacher from a Higher Realm

She avoided him. They all avoided him.

Lan didn't look up from her dictionary when he spoke to her.

Jamie, a supportive collar of foam around his neck, kept a wary distance.

His mother, drifting like a pale ghost through the house,
was afraid to address him in case he snapped at her again
to go and get a life.

KEVIN felt **miserable.**

Finally he was powerful, strong, the way he had always wished to be, and people feared him.
The only person who grinned to see him was Avatar.

Together, they ranged around the cyber world on the back of the dragon. Only
something was wrong with the pixel colouring. The scarlet and gold had turned grey.
Kevin knew that if he were to reach inside the dragon's mouth there would be no jewel
gleaming beneath its tongue.

Jamaster's realm had been destroyed. All other missions
seemed hollow. Princess Lana seemed more and more like
a doll, hollowly carrying out his commands.

Reading Between the Lines

Why does the cyber world
lose its colour for Kevin
and depict missions that
seem "hollow"? What
inferences can you make
about this?

Kevin felt cheated. Lan was supposed to be
impressed by his transformation. She was
supposed to fall in love with him.

He found her in the school library and tried
one last time. "Why won't you speak to me?"

Lan looked up over her dictionary and gazed
at him searchingly. "You aren't who I thought
you were."

"But what do you mean?" Kevin asked
in frustration.

24

"I thought you were kind and I liked that."
She shuddered. "But then you changed.
What you did to Jamie. You scared me.
My family, too."

Unable to look her in the eye, Kevin idly
flicked through the dictionary: avarice,
avascular, avast…

"But I stopped them from picking on us."

Avatar. 1. Manifestation of a deity in
superhuman form. 2. A teacher from
a higher realm.

Lan nodded grimly. "My family believes
there should always be other ways than
violence."

Although she did not say it, Kevin
remembered Lan's earlier words.
"My brother stepped on a landmine."

He looked at her intently. "What if I
change back to who I was? What if I show
you who I really am?"

Lan smiled. "I'd like that a lot."

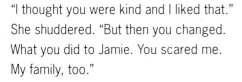

what if I show you
who I really am

Issues ✕ Is violence an issue in your community? What is your opinion about meeting violence with violence?

25

Victory

This time, the start-up hum of the computer filled Kevin with dread. He tasted metallic fear in his mouth as he typed in the name of the game.

Avatar appeared with his sword, grinning.

"I'm sorry," Kevin whispered, "but I need to get the girl."

Avatar mounted the dragon, its scales gleaming scarlet and gold once more. "Mission?" he asked in his mechanical tone.

Kevin sighed. "Anywhere," he typed.

Avatar waited, his expression blank. "Who are our enemies in Anywhere?"

"There are **NO MORE** enemies."

Author Purpose

Why do you think the author wrote this story? What messages does the author convey to the reader?

"Where is Anywhere?" Avatar droned.

Kevin thought about Lan and her family and how, after this was done, he would go to the restaurant. He would help her grandmother shell prawns and laugh with her cousins. He would feel safe showing them all who he really was. Lan would learn that, deep down, he could be trusted. It might take weeks, months. But then, one day, one special day, they would kiss beneath the sparkling mirror that kept rival dragons out…

"Far, far away." Kevin typed. He watched Avatar leap upon the dragon and fly into a purple swirl of clouds.

Kevin pulled the heavy curtain away from his window. Golden afternoon light sifted through the dusty panes. Outside, Mrs Azzapardi chatted with Mrs Delaney while her yappy dog turned somersaults around them.

Smiling, Kevin clicked:

PROGRAM
UNINSTALL.

Question Generate

What questions could be asked about this text?

Think about the Text

MAKING CONNECTIONS

What connections can you make to the characters, plot, setting and themes of **Avatar**?

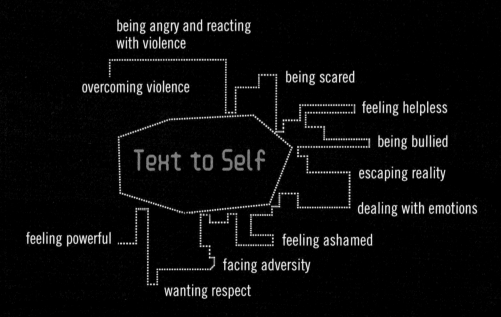

being angry and reacting with violence

overcoming violence

being scared

feeling helpless

being bullied

Text to Self

escaping reality

dealing with emotions

feeling powerful

feeling ashamed

facing adversity

wanting respect

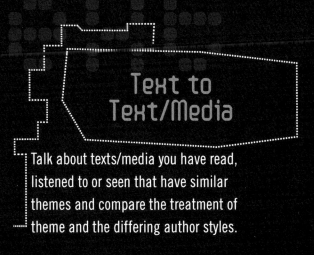

Text to Text/Media

Talk about texts/media you have read, listened to or seen that have similar themes and compare the treatment of theme and the differing author styles.

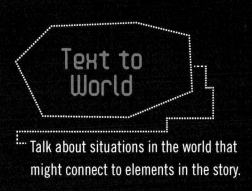

Text to World

Talk about situations in the world that might connect to elements in the story.

Planning a Contemporary Fiction

Contemporary fiction incorporates many different genres,
such as mystery, science fiction, adventure, narrative, recount...

1 Think about what **defines** contemporary fiction

Contemporary fiction connects the reader with the complex situations and events
of contemporary society. It incorporates themes and contexts that are seen as:

- A REFLECTION OF THE PAST
  - A MIRROR OF THE PRESENT
    - AN INDICATOR OF THE FUTURE.

2 Think about the **plot**

Decide on a plot that has an introduction, problems and a solution, and write
them in the order of sequence.

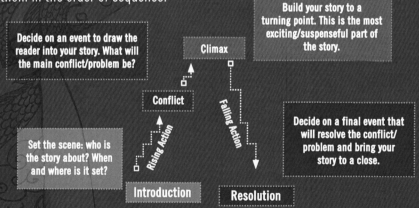

Build your story to a
turning point. This is the most
exciting/suspenseful part of
the story.

Decide on an event to draw the
reader into your story. What will
the main conflict/problem be?

Climax

Conflict

Decide on a final event that
will resolve the conflict/
problem and bring your
story to a close.

Set the scene: who is
the story about? When
and where is it set?

Rising Action

Falling Action

Introduction

Resolution

Think about the sequence of events and how to present them using contemporary fiction
devices, such as *flashback* and *foreshadowing*.

Flashback = showing part of the storyline out of sequence.

Foreshadowing = suggesting or indicating events before they happen.

3 Think about **the characters**

Explore:

- how they think, feel and act
  - what motivates their behaviour
    - their inner feelings, using contemporary fiction approaches, such as stream of consciousness and product-of-society typecasting.

> stream of consciousness = a description of the flow of thoughts and feelings through a character's mind as they arise
>
> product-of-society typecasting = giving the characters roles that are typical of the society they were born into

4 Decide on **the setting**

atmosphere/
mood   location   time

> Note: Contemporary fiction provides a window into current lifestyles and living conditions, which are often shaped by multimedia influences.

Writing a Contemporary Fiction

Have you…

- Made links to the society and events of your period?

- Identified with recurrent contemporary themes?

- Maintained a fast pace of action?

- Grabbed the readers' attention and dragged them from the first page to the final page?

- Been true to the context of your time frame?

- Provided a window on the past or present or future?

- Explored contemporary values and beliefs?

- Developed characters that will stand up to in-depth analysis?

…DON'T FORGET TO REVISIT YOUR WRITING.

DO YOU NEED TO CHANGE, ADD OR DELETE ANYTHING TO IMPROVE YOUR STORY?